Tornadoes

Ted O'Hare

FITZGERALD BOOKS

Bethany, Missouri

Photo Credits:
Cover © Sean Martin; Title Page © Nathan Holland; Page 5 © Anita Colic; Page 6 © Bent G. Nordeng; Page 7
© Jessica Bethke; Page 9 © Jonathan Lenz; Page 11 © Allyson Ricketts; Page 12 © Clint Spencer,
Vladimir Kondrachov; Page 13 © Lawrence Sawyer; Page 15 © Graham Prentice; Page 16 © Peter Molnar;
Page 17 © Bill Grove; Page 19 © NOAA; Page 21 © David Brimm; Page 22 © Mark Wolfe/FEMA News Photo

Cataloging-in-Publication Data

O'Hare, Ted, 1961-
    Tornadoes / Ted O'Hare. — 1st ed.
    p. cm. — (Natural disasters)

    Includes bibliographical references and index.
    Summary: Illustrations and text introduce tornadoes, from
what causes them, to how they are measured, tracked, and predicted.
    ISBN-13: 978-1-4242-1402-0 (lib. bdg. : alk. paper)
    ISBN-10: 1-4242-1402-5 (lib. bdg. : alk. paper)
    ISBN-13: 978-1-4242-1492-1 (pbk. : alk. paper)
    ISBN-10: 1-4242-1492-0 (pbk. : alk. paper)

    1. Tornadoes—Juvenile literature. [1. Tornadoes.
2. Natural disasters.] I. O'Hare, Ted, 1961- II. Title.
III. Series.
    QC955.2.O43 2007
    551.55'3—dc22

First edition
© 2007 Fitzgerald Books
802 N. 41st Street, P.O. Box 505
Bethany, MO 64424, U.S.A.
Printed in China
Library of Congress Control Number: 2006911280

Table of Contents

What Makes a Tornado?

A tornado is the strongest windstorm. A tornado is mostly seen as a moving **column** of air that extends from a cloud to the ground.

This column is known as a **funnel cloud**. A funnel cloud becomes a tornado only when it touches the ground.

Tornadoes happen when warm, moist air rises to meet cool, dry air.

Most dangerous tornadoes form from very large thunderstorms known as **supercells**. Supercells can produce lightning, heavy rains, flooding, hail, and strong winds.

United States of America

South Dakota

Minnesota

Iowa

Nebraska

Colorado

Kansas

Oklahoma

Texas

☐ Tornado Alley

Tornadoes can happen anywhere, but mostly they are seen in the United States. In fact, one area of the central plains is known as Tornado Alley. Generally, more than a thousand tornadoes are recorded every year.

Peak tornado season is in the spring and summer. Most tornadoes develop in late afternoon or early evening. Tornadoes are often the product of a hurricane.

Tornadoes come in many shapes, sizes, and colors. Many are wide at the top and narrow at the bottom. But some are as wide as they are tall. Colors can sometimes change when a tornado picks up **debris** as it moves along.

Sometimes tornadoes are so **compact** that a house on one side of a street will be totally destroyed, whereas the one across from it remains untouched.

Measuring Tornadoes

Some tornadoes are weak, and some are strong. Tornadoes can be measured on a list known as the Fujita Scale. This scale estimates a storm's wind speed.

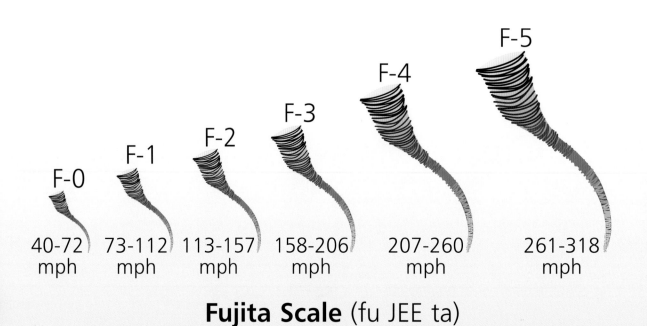

F-0 — 40-72 mph

F-1 — 73-112 mph

F-2 — 113-157 mph

F-3 — 158-206 mph

F-4 — 207-260 mph

F-5 — 261-318 mph

Fujita Scale (fu JEE ta)

Waterspouts

A waterspout is a tornado over water. Waterspouts are not as strong as tornadoes, but they can be dangerous to boats, swimmers, and even airplanes. The Florida Keys can have up to 400 waterspouts in a year.

Keeping Track of Tornadoes

Storm spotters often "chase" storms. They may be **meteorologists** or they may not be. They may be people who want to learn more about tornadoes by studying them. Some people chase storms for the thrill of it.

Predicting Tornadoes

Modern technology gives meteorologists better advance warning about tornadoes. Meteorologists use **Doppler** radar to learn about how strong a thunderstorm is. Doppler shows if the speed of wind blowing around rainfall is strong enough to become a tornado.

21

The Storm Prediction Center (SPC) is located in Oklahoma. Scientists at this center can forecast severe weather. The information they gather gives us earlier storm warnings.

Glossary

column (KALL um) — a vertical mass

compact (kom PAKT) — concentrated; focused

debris (DEB ree) — things on the ground

Doppler (DOPP lur) — a radar device that measures the amount of precipitation and its movement

funnel cloud (FUN nul CLOWD) — a cloud shaped like a funnel

meteorologist (MEE tee uh rol uh jist) — a scientist trained in weather and climate

supercell (SOO pur sell) — the strongest type of thunderstorm

Index

FURTHER READING

Osborne, Will and Mary Pope. *Twisters and Other Terrible Storms*. Scholastic, 2003.
Thomas, Rick. *Twisters: A Book About Tornadoes.* Picture Window Books, 2005.
White, Matt. *Storm Chasers: On the Trail of Deadly Tornadoes.* Capstone Press, 2003.

WEBSITES TO VISIT

Because Internet links change so often, Fitzgerald Books has developed an online list of websites related to the subject of this book. This site is updated regularly. Please use this link to access the list: www.fitzgeraldbookslinks.com/nd/tor

ABOUT THE AUTHOR

Ted O'Hare is an author and editor of children's nonfiction books. Ted has written over fifty children's books over the past decade. Ted has worked for many publishing houses including the Macmillan Children's Book Group.